WITCH
IN TRAINING

For Rob, Cori and Dudley
M.R.

For Jane, Mike, Dan and George
B.M.S.

WALKER BOOKS
AND SUBSIDIARIES
LONDON · BOSTON · SYDNEY · AUCKLAND

WITCH
IN TRAINING

Michelle Robinson   Briony May Smith

My cauldron training starts tonight!
I hope I get my potions right.

Mum is helping. *"First things first:*

*you'll need a wand
that's nice and cursed.*

*Which potion would
you like to brew?"*

I pick one out for
Magic Stew.

The list of what we need
is whopping.

"*Grab your broomstick,*   *let's go shopping!*"

My kitten comes as well.
"Let's fly!"   And off we zoom …

into the sky.

Raindrops, moonbeams, lightning bolts. The recipe
says sixty volts.

My kitten's whiskers start to smoke.
"Quick, Pumpkin Patch, climb in my cloak!"

"*We may as well stock up on things,*"
my mum says. "*Dust from fairy wings,*

some phoenix feathers,

dragonflies,

*plus owl earwax –
jumbo size."*

I fill four jars then
we fly down …

to fetch supplies from Monster Town!
Werewolf whiskers, zombie brains,

troll hair plucked from filthy drains.

Mum says, "Well, so far so good.
We've done the sky, ticked off the wood…"

I can't squeeze much more on my broom!
But now we're visiting ...

a tomb!

Mum reads, *"Thigh bones,*

mummy dust,

ghostly chains,
complete with rust."

I check the list.
We're still not through…

Next up: vampire fangs,
times two.

I beg Mum, "Can I get a rat?"

My new pet crawls
inside my hat.

He nestles down in
my long hair.

I soon forget he's
even there.

Just one more stop:
the local jetty...

"Nice sea monster – come to Betty!"

Mum says, "My, you have done well.
Now let's head home and start your spell."

I've checked my wand. I've read the book.
I've even washed my hands, Mum — look!

Pumpkin Patch thinks I can do it!
Piece of cake, there's nothing to it.

I wave my wand!

I stir my brew! I say the magic words ...

Then Mum points out
the small print.

PLEASE,
when mixing potions,
DO NOT SNEEZE.

Pumpkin Patch is now a frog!
I wave my wand...

A horse!

A dog?!

A giant butterfly?!
Oh, no!

But I can make *more* potion, so...
Abracadabra!

Mum says, "*Wow!*
Pumpkin's back to normal!"
MIAOW!

I'm glad my little cat's OK.
It's been the most exhausting day.
Mum tucks me in when I start yawning.

"You'll need a new spell in the morning..."

Oh, toadstools! How could I forget?
I need to fix my other pet!